Fairy Tale Science

# Making a Raft for the Three Billy Goats Gruff

by Sue Gagliardi

# www.focusreaders.com

Copyright © 2020 by Focus Readers®, Lake Elmo, MN 55042. All rights reserved. No part of this book may be reproduced or utilized in any form or by any means without written permission from the publisher.

Focus Readers is distributed by North Star Editions:
sales@northstareditions.com | 888-417-0195

Produced for Focus Readers by Red Line Editorial.

Photographs ©: The Protected Art Archive/Alamy, cover (left), 1 (left); Red Line Editorial, cover (right), 1 (right), 11, 13, 15, 25, 27; Svetlana123/iStockphoto, 4; jmagfoto/Shutterstock Images, 7, 29; shuttertoyz/Shutterstock Images, 8; Mark Green/Alamy, 16–17; gosphotodesign/Shutterstock Images, 18; ForeverLee/Shutterstock Images, 21; Noam Armonn/Shutterstock Images, 22

### Library of Congress Cataloging-in-Publication Data
Library of Congress Cataloging-in-Publication Data is available on the Library of Congress website.

### ISBN
978-1-64493-030-4 (hardcover)
978-1-64493-109-7 (paperback)
978-1-64493-267-4 (ebook pdf)
978-1-64493-188-2 (hosted ebook)

Printed in the United States of America
Mankato, MN
012020

# About the Author

Sue Gagliardi writes fiction, nonfiction, and poetry for children. Her books include *Fairies, Get Outside in Winter*, and *Get Outside in Spring*. Her work appears in children's magazines including *Highlights Hello, Highlights High Five, Ladybug*, and *Spider*. She teaches kindergarten and lives in Pennsylvania with her husband and son.

# Table of Contents

**CHAPTER 1**
## The Three Billy Goats Gruff  5

**CHAPTER 2**
## Build a Raft  9

▶ **IN THE REAL WORLD**
## The Amazon International Raft Race  16

**CHAPTER 3**
## Results  19

**CHAPTER 4**
## The Science of Rafts  23

Focus on Making a Raft • 28
Glossary • 30
To Learn More • 31
Index • 32

# Chapter 1

# The Three Billy Goats Gruff

Three billy goats came to a bridge. A hungry troll lived under the bridge. The smallest goat tried to cross first. The troll wanted to eat the goat. But the goat convinced the troll to wait.

➤ **A billy goat is a male. Females are known as nanny goats.**

He told the troll that his older brother would be coming soon. His brother was bigger. He would be a tastier meal. The greedy troll agreed to wait. And the smallest goat crossed the bridge safely.

The medium-sized goat tried to cross next. He also convinced the hungry troll to wait. The troll let the medium-sized goat cross the bridge.

The largest goat came last. He charged at the troll. The troll fell

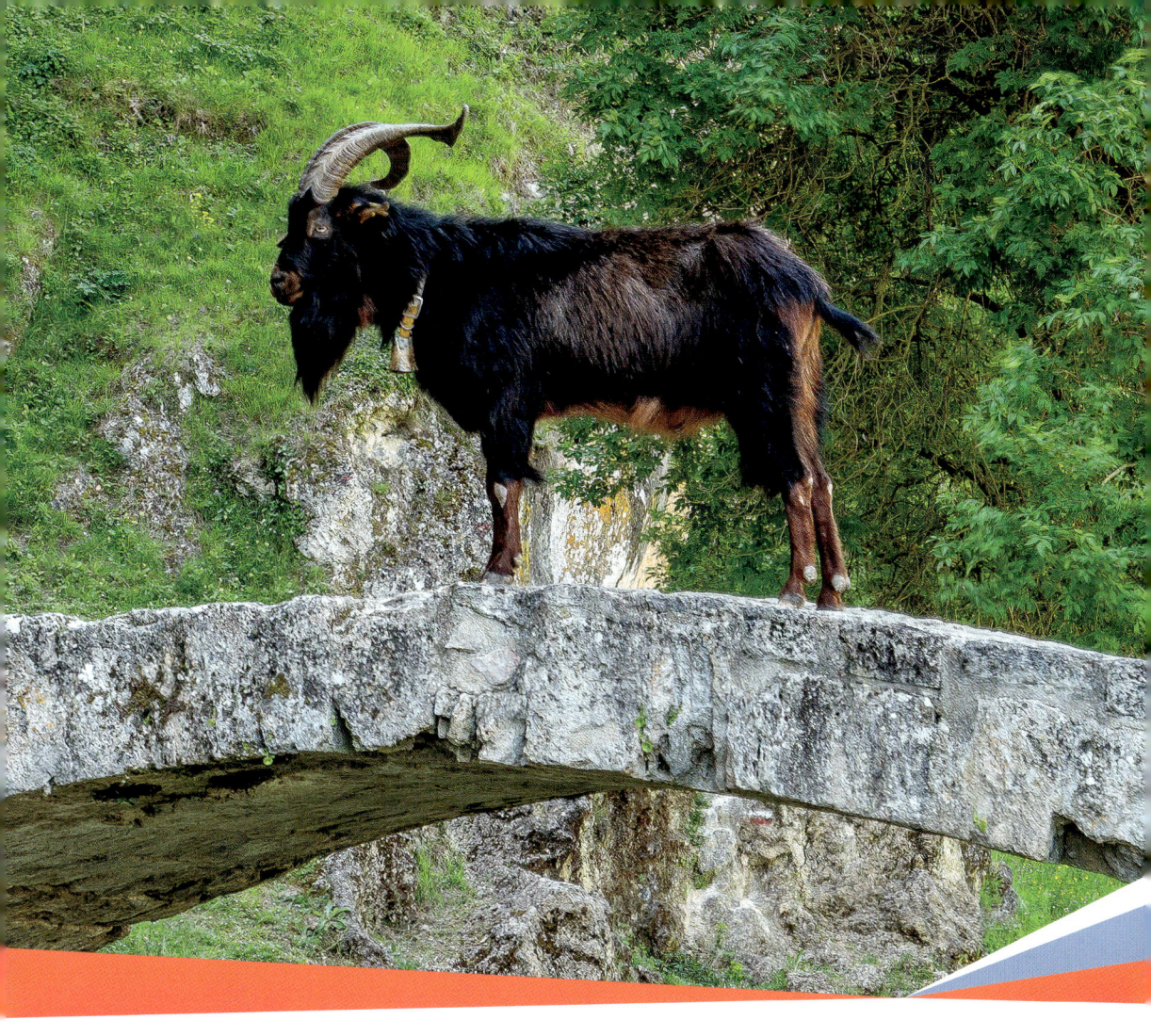

> The goats were able to trick the troll and cross the bridge.

into the water. The largest goat crossed the bridge. The goats were safe from the hungry troll.

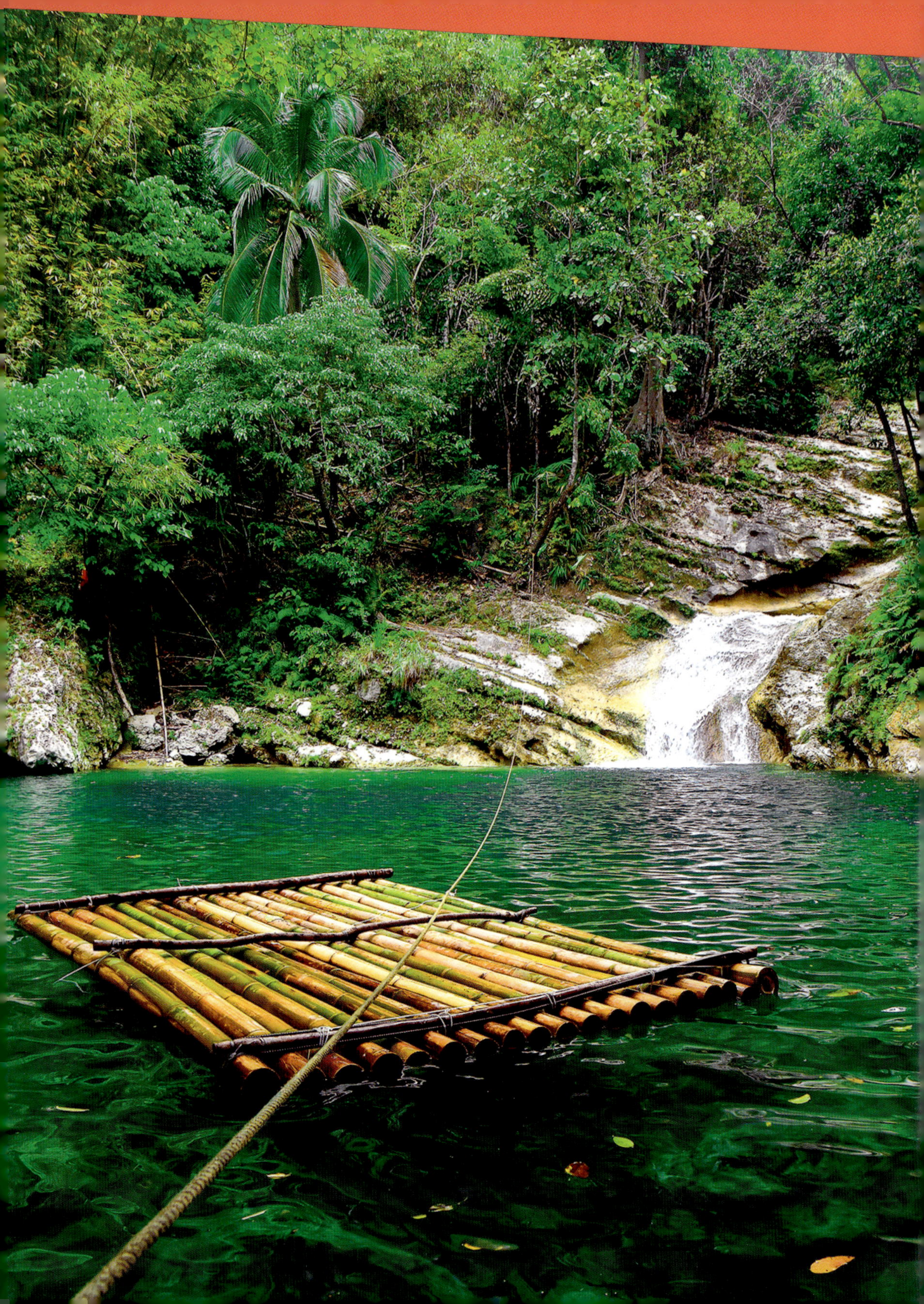

## Chapter 2

# Build a Raft

To cross the bridge, the goats had to be smarter than the troll. They used his greed against him. But the goats also could have **avoided** the troll. They could have crossed the river using a raft.

> A raft is a flat structure that floats on water.

You will create a raft for the goats. The raft should be strong enough to hold at least 20 grams of **mass**. It should also float for at least one minute. You will test three different **models**. The models will be made of straws, sticks, and a sponge.

## Materials

- 5 plastic straws, cut in half
- 4 pipe cleaners
- 5 wooden craft sticks
- 1 kitchen sponge

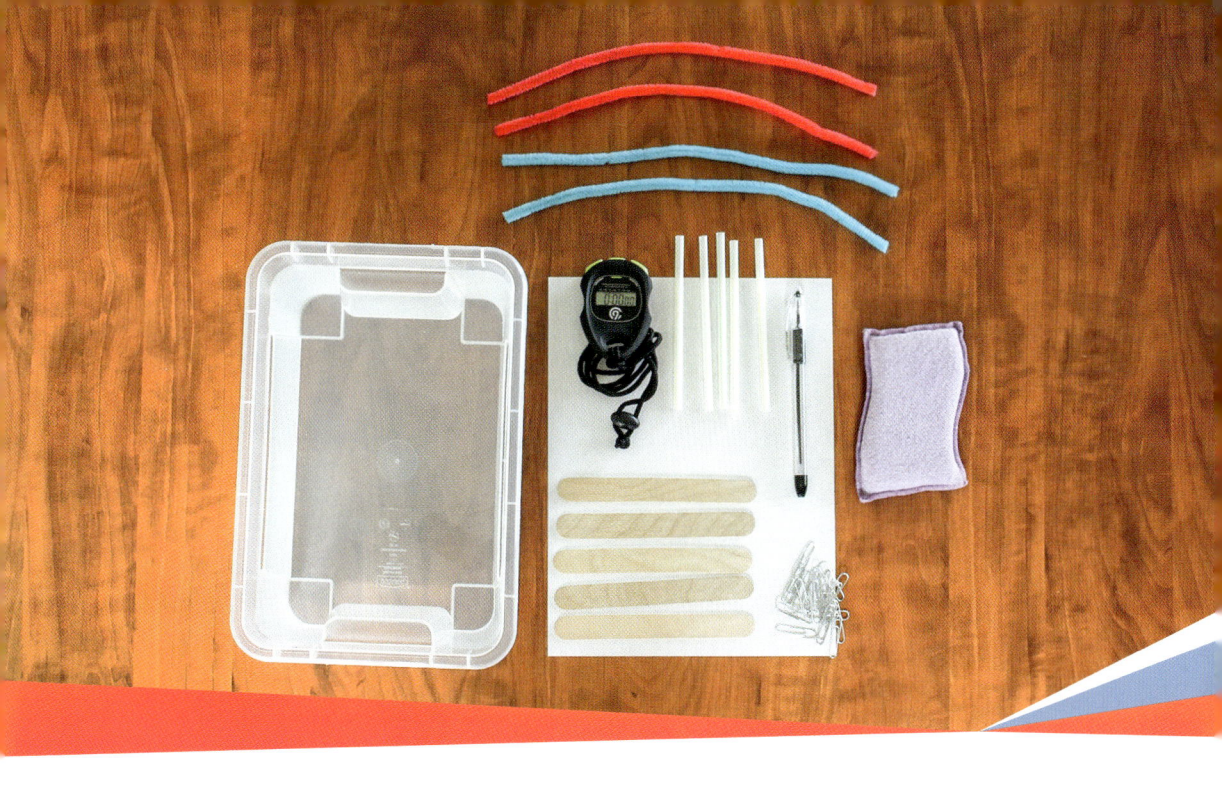

- 20 large paper clips, equaling approximately 20 grams of mass
- Stopwatch
- Large, rectangular container filled with water
- Paper and pen/pencil

## Instructions

**Making the Rafts**

1. Make the straw raft. First, line up the straws side by side. Next, use two pipe cleaners to hold the straws together. Bend one pipe cleaner around each end of the straws. The straws should lie flat.

**Fun Fact**

Marine engineers design and build boats for their job.

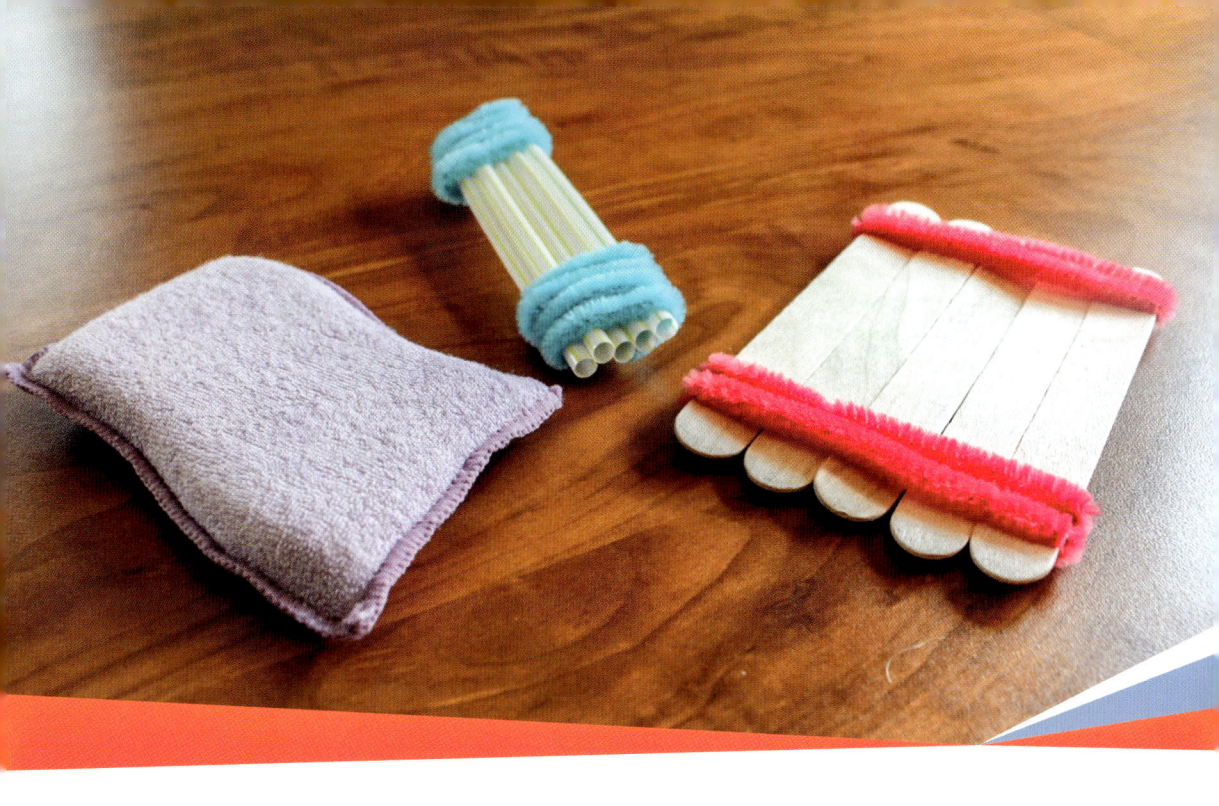

2. Make the stick raft. First, line up the sticks side by side. Next, use two pipe cleaners to hold the sticks together. The sticks should lie flat.

3. The kitchen sponge will be the final raft.

## Testing the Rafts

1. Place the straw raft in the water.
2. Add two paper clips to the raft.
3. Start the stopwatch.
4. If the raft is still floating after 10 seconds, add two more paper clips to the raft. Keep adding paper clips until the raft begins to sink.
5. Repeat steps 2 through 4 for three **trials**. Time how long the raft floats in each trial. How many paper clips could the raft

hold? Write down the results of each trial.

6. Repeat steps 1 through 5 using the stick raft.

7. Repeat steps 1 through 5 using the sponge raft.

**IN THE REAL WORLD**

# The Amazon International Raft Race

The world's longest raft race takes place in Peru. People from all over the world compete. Teams of four people build their own rafts. They use rope, nails, and eight wooden logs. Then they paddle through the rainforest. They race along the Amazon River. It is one of the world's longest rivers. The teams stop to eat meals. They sleep in tents. Then they continue the race. It lasts for three days. Teams paddle 118 miles (190 km) to reach the finish line.

*Teams paddle down the Amazon during the race.*

17

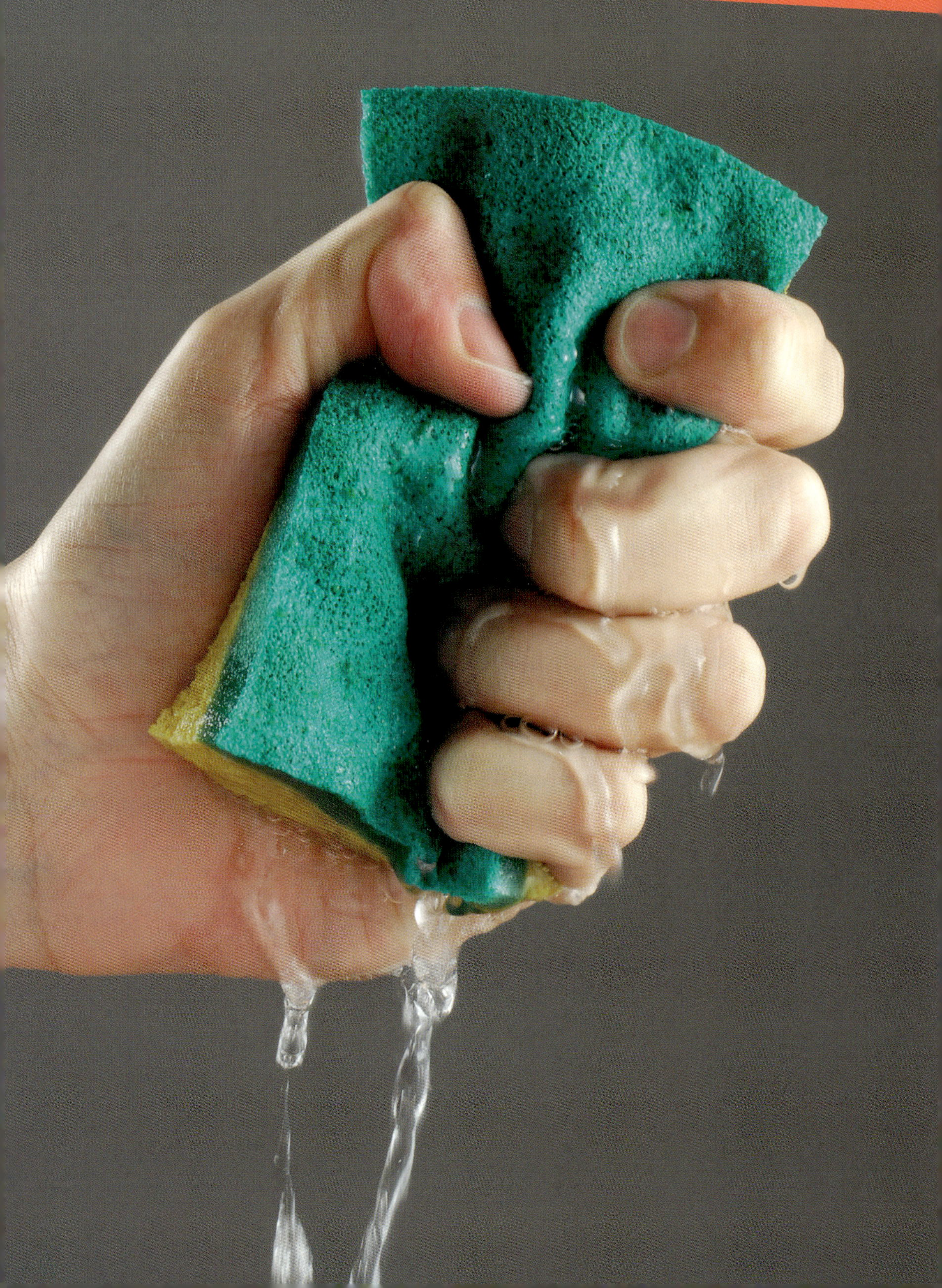

# Chapter 3

# Results

All three rafts can hold 20 grams of mass. But each of them will sink if enough mass is added. Also, the sponge **absorbs** water. That added weight will contribute to the sponge sinking.

▶ Sponges get heavier as they soak up water.

Adjust your models to help them hold even more mass. Try some of these ideas:

- Add more straws or sticks to make the rafts wider.
- Try making a raft out of different materials. Think about which materials float best.

### Fun Fact

Cork is a material that floats well. It has tiny holes that trap air. The air helps it float.

> **Cork and wood float because they have many tiny air bubbles in them.**

- Cover the straw raft with plastic wrap. The wrap will keep the water out.

Which raft holds the most mass? Which raft floats the longest?

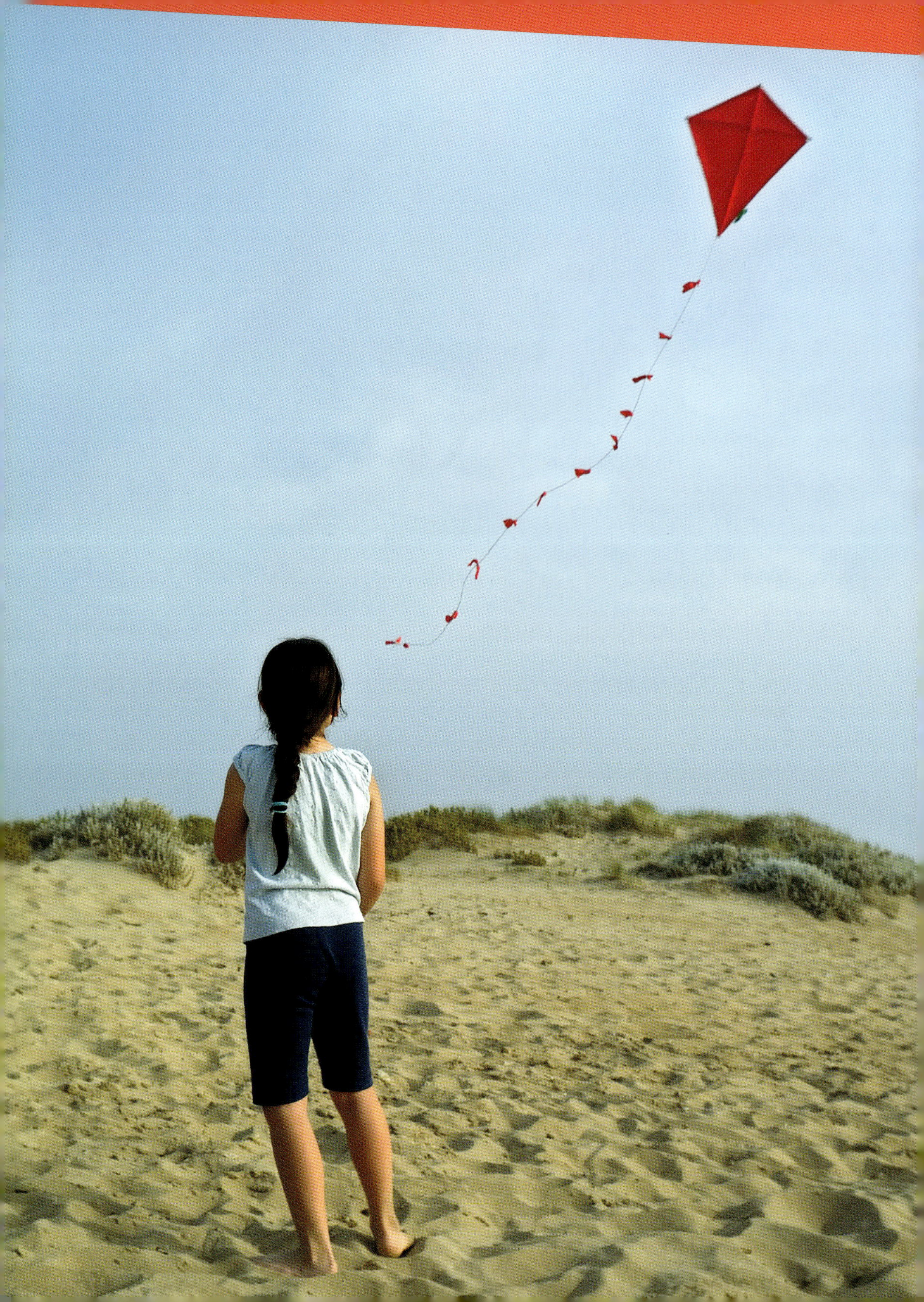

# Chapter 4

# The Science of Rafts

All objects are made of **matter**. **Density** is a measure of how much matter is in a given space. It measures how heavy an object is compared to its size.

▶ People, sand, and even air are made of matter.

Some objects are made of loosely packed matter. These objects have low density. Other objects are made of tightly packed matter. They have a higher density. Objects float when they are less dense than water. Objects sink when they are denser than water.

**Fun Fact**

Submarines are ships that can move underwater. They have tanks. They float when the tanks fill up with air. They sink when the tanks fill up with water.

# MATTER AND DENSITY

A beach ball is filled with air. The matter in air is loosely packed. The beach ball floats on water.

Water

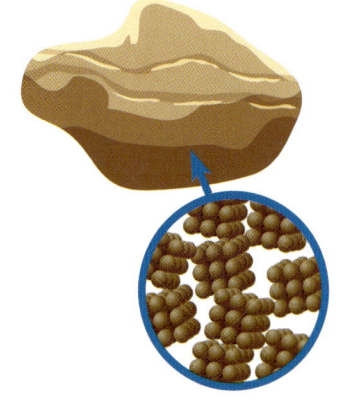

The matter in this rock is tightly packed. The rock will sink in water.

An object's **surface area** also determines whether it will float. An object in water displaces the water. The object pushes water aside.

The water pushes against the object with a **force** called **buoyancy**. This force holds the object up.

Think about swimming in a pool. A swimmer floats when she stretches out flat on the water. She is increasing her surface area. The swimmer sinks when she curls into a ball. She is decreasing her surface

**Fun Fact**

Ships float higher in seawater than in fresh water. Salt makes seawater denser.

# BUOYANCY AND SURFACE AREA

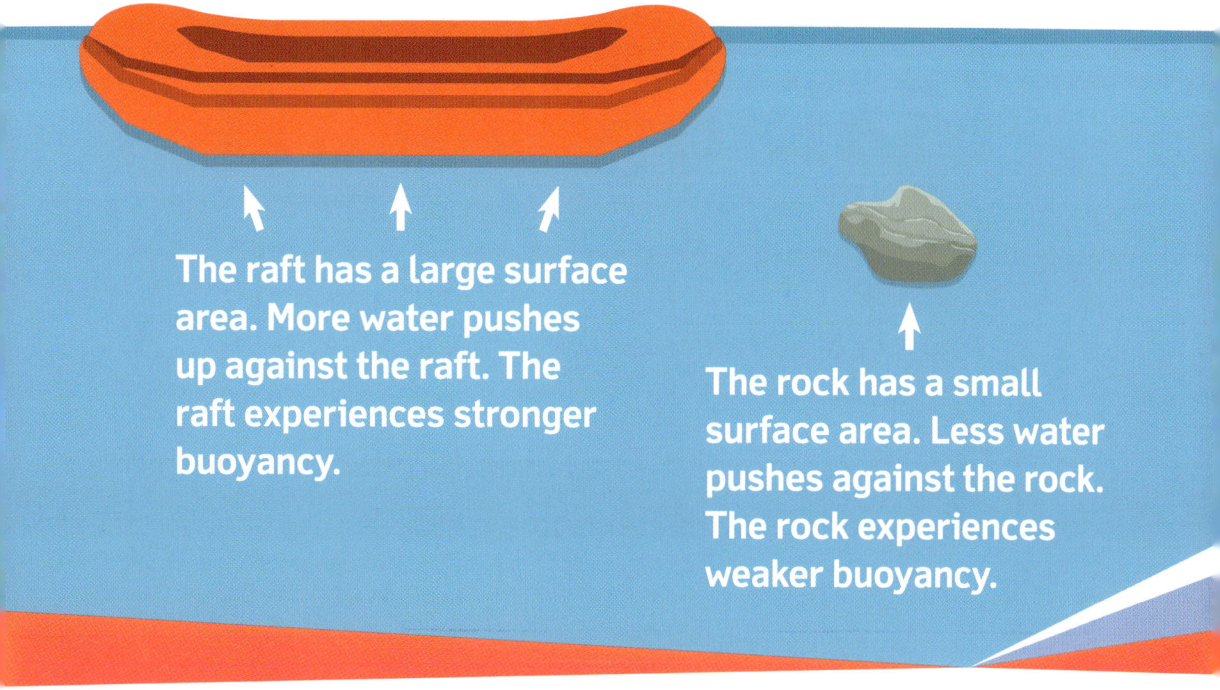

The raft has a large surface area. More water pushes up against the raft. The raft experiences stronger buoyancy.

The rock has a small surface area. Less water pushes against the rock. The rock experiences weaker buoyancy.

area. There is less surface area for the water to push up against.

A successful raft is less dense than water. It is also wide and flat. It has a large surface area. A raft can help the goats avoid the troll.

## FOCUS ON
# Making a Raft

*Write your answers on a separate piece of paper.*

1. Write a paragraph summarizing the key points of Chapter 4.

2. Why do you think it's important to do more than one trial when testing a model?

3. Objects with a higher density than water will do what?
   - **A.** sink in the water
   - **B.** float on the water
   - **C.** be more buoyant

4. Why would making a raft wider help it float better?
   - **A.** The raft's surface area decreases.
   - **B.** The raft becomes denser than water.
   - **C.** The raft's surface area increases.

**5.** What does **convinced** mean in this book?

*But the goat **convinced** the troll to wait. He told the troll that his older brother would be coming soon. His brother was bigger. He would be a tastier meal.*

    **A.** caused someone to doubt information
    **B.** caused someone to believe information
    **C.** caused someone to ask questions

**6.** What does **displaces** mean in this book?

*An object in water **displaces** the water. The object pushes water aside.*

    **A.** causes something to stay in one place
    **B.** causes something to get bigger
    **C.** causes something to move from its place

*Answer key on page 32.*

# Glossary

**absorbs**
Soaks up a liquid.

**avoided**
Stayed away from something.

**buoyancy**
A force that pushes up on objects in water.

**density**
A measure of how many particles are packed into a certain amount of space.

**force**
A push or pull that one object has on another.

**mass**
The amount of matter in an object.

**matter**
Anything that has mass and takes up space.

**models**
Small copies of a real object.

**surface area**
A measurement of the total area covered by the surface of an object.

**trials**
Tests to see if something is working.

# To Learn More

## BOOKS

Hestermann, Josh, and Bethanie Hestermann. *Marine Science for Kids: Exploring and Protecting Our Watery World*. Chicago: Chicago Review Press, 2017.

Polinsky, Paige V. *Super Simple Experiments with Mass: Fun and Innovative Science Projects*. Minneapolis: Abdo Publishing, 2017.

Swanson, Jennifer. *Explore Forces and Motion!* White River Junction, VT: Nomad Press, 2016.

## NOTE TO EDUCATORS

Visit **www.focusreaders.com** to find lesson plans, activities, links, and other resources related to this title.

# Index

## A
Amazon International Raft Race, 16

## B
billy goats, 5–7, 9–10, 27
buoyancy, 26–27

## D
density, 23–25

## F
force, 26

## M
mass, 10–11, 19–21
matter, 23–25

## S
submarines, 24
surface area, 25–27

Answer Key: 1. Answers will vary; 2. Answers will vary; 3. A; 4. C; 5. B; 6. C